METAL MAN

Aaron Reynolds

Illustrated by Paul Hoppe

ini Charlesbridge

Summer's hangin' on
like a big ol' bear,
stickin' on the city, cookin' it good.
And I'm headin' over to see the metal man.
"Where you goin', Devon?"
It's my little sister, Asia.
"You know where," I say.
She don't follow, 'cause she's scared of the noise.
But I ain't.

His name's Mitch, but I don't call him that.
He's got his green metal door
slid up and open
like a big ol' dragon mouth.
Sparks are flyin'.
It's all loud and grindy,
and I know the metal man's workin'.

"Whatcha makin', Metal Man?" I say.

He don't answer. He never does.

"Whaddya see?" That's all he says.

It don't look like nothin' yet.

But he pulls out his fire torch.

It howls like the El train comin'.

And he starts meltin' metal pieces on.

They stick,
hot and red,
like my sweaty back on the plastic bus seats,
cookin' together.
Sweat's pourin' down the metal man,
but he don't stop.

Mama says the metal man ain't really workin'.

"That ain't art," she says. "It's junk.

Makin' junk out of junk ain't a real job."

But I don't know. Looks like work to me.

"I see a heart," I say.

"Yup," he says. "What else?"

"A spiderweb, all sticky and long," I tell him.

"Is that right?"

The metal man stares at me, hard and strong.

"Is that what you see?" he asks me.

"Uh-huh."

"Then it's right."

When I hang out with the metal man, I get it right.

I see what I see.

Not like school.

"Can I try somethin'?" I ask.

He don't even answer.

He don't have to.

"That torch'll tear you up like a thousand killer bees.

You don't mess with that," he always says.

But today he looks over at me. "Whaddya wanna make?"

He ain't never said that before.

I think real hard, eyes gritted up tight.

I got a spark in my head, but I ain't sayin' it with my mouth.

"I don't know," I say.

It's a lie, but I tell it anyway.

"Yeah, you do," he says.

"Don't be scared, boy. Bring it on out to play."

That metal man can see inside me like glass.

"I wanna make a house in a star," I say.

"You wanna live in a star?" that metal man asks.

"Maybe," I say back all mad and growly, 'cause I know it's dumb.

"That's cool," he says. "Let's make that star-house."

He picks some metal out of the heap,

all covered with scuzz,

and heads over to the big ol' saw with the barbed-wire blade.

He looks back at me, that metal man.

"You comin'?" he asks. "It's your star-house."

He yanks out his deep-sea goggles,
two sets this time,
and we squeeze 'em on.
Then that saw starts squealin',
and I feel it cuttin' into my metal,
like a shark on a fish,
grindin' through it with those teeth.

We cut and cut,

star-fronts, star-backs, star-sides.

It ain't much yet, but that's OK.

"What's the house look like?" he asks me.

"I don't know," I say.

"Yeah, you do," he says back.

"Draw it out in your head,

and tell me how it goes."

There's a chimney,

and some windows,

and a round door.

I tell it all, and the metal man cuts out the pieces.

"You stand back now," he says. "Killer bees, remember?"
That angry fire kicks up out of his torch,
burnin' together
windows and doors and sides
of a star-house I made in my head.

I thought it was dumb at first,
but that fire torch don't think it's dumb.
It looks glad, I think,
sizzlin' all fiery and fierce.

He turns off the fire with a chuff.
The metal's all charred and black and burnt,
but that's OK,
'cause I know the grinder's comin'.
I know what's hidin' underneath the crud.
He digs in,
sendin' sparks everywhere,
and that metal starts shinin'
all silver and blue.
It was under there all the time.

Summer's fryin' up the block outside.
But I'm seein' silver hearts
and spiderwebs
and my very own star-house,
comin' together in the metal man's sparks.

I know what Mama says,
but it don't look like junk to me,
all shiny and ferocious.

Back home Asia's yellin' at a dog,

and I'm slippin' in,

quiet and soft.

"Hey, Son, where you been?"

It's Mama.

"You know where," I say.

"What's the junk man makin' today?" she asks.

Part of me don't wanna show, but I gotta.

There's a fire in me, just like that torch.

"This," I say, bringing out my shinin' silver thing.

Mama looks hard,

turnin' it up and down.

"It's got your name on the back. You make this?"

"Kinda," I say. I'm sweatin' outside,

but my breath feels icy inside me.

"Outta junk?" she asks.

"Yep," I say.

She klunks it down on the air conditioner,

that place where everybody hangs out.

"Well, it sure ain't junk now," says Mama.

Summer's cookin' the streets outside,
bakin' 'em black.
But everything's cool and comfy
inside by the silver star.

I'm seein' things different,
and maybe Mama is too,
all because of that fiery metal man.

To Mitch Levin,

the real metal man,

who continues to inspire me

and to Susie, Zane, and Maddie,

who put up with him

—A. R.

For my father—P. H.

Text copyright © 2008 by Aaron Reynolds
Illustrations copyright © 2008 by Paul Hoppe
All rights reserved, including the right of reproduction in whole or in part
in any form. Charlesbridge and colophon are registered trademarks of
Charlesbridge Publishing, Inc.

Published by Charlesbridge
85 Main Street
Watertown, MA 02472
(617) 926-0329
www.charlesbridge.com

Library of Congress Cataloging-in-Publication Data
Reynolds, Aaron, 1970–
   Metal man / Aaron Reynolds ; illustrated by Paul Hoppe.
     p. cm.
   Summary: One hot summer day, a man who makes sculpture out of
junk helps a boy create what he sees in his mind's eye.
   ISBN 978-1-58089-150-9 (reinforced for library use)
[1. Junk sculpture—Fiction. 2. Metalwork—Fiction.
3. African Americans—Fiction.] I. Hoppe, Paul, ill. II. Title.
PZ7.R33213Me 2008
[Fic]—dc22   2007017187

Printed in China
(hc) 10 9 8 7 6 5 4 3 2 1

Illustrations done in mixed media
Display type handlettered by Paul Hoppe
   and text type set in Sabon
Color preparation by Chroma Graphics, Singapore
Printed and bound by Jade Productions
Production supervision by Brian G. Walker
Designed by Susan Mallory Sherman